1 2 3 4 5 6 7 8 9 10

First Edition

STUART LITTLE™

A Little Mess

Adaptation by Laura Driscoll

Based on the teleplay "Adventures in Housekeeping"

by Rob Hoegee

Illustrations by Jose Lopez

HarperFestival®

A Division of HarperCollinsPublishers

It was Saturday morning
at the Little house.
The Littles had just given
Snowbell a bath when . . .

Ah-CHOO!

Mrs. Little sneezed a big sneeze.

She was wet.

She was shivering.

She had a cold!

So Mr. Little put Mrs. Little to bed.

"But it's Saturday," said Mrs. Little.

"I always do my weekly housekeeping
and go to the market on Saturday."

Mrs. Little wanted the house
to look its best.

After all, Stuart and George had
entered it in the local
"Home of the Year" contest.

"The kids and I will take care of everything!" said Mr. Little.

Together, they set out to do

the Saturday chores.

First, they went grocery
shopping.

Then they made lunch and fed Martha.
Sort of.

Stuart watered the plants—

and George and Mr. Little!

They loaded the dishwasher.

"I added the soap," said Stuart.

"*You* added the soap?" asked George.

"But *I* added the soap!"

"Me, too," exclaimed Mr. Little.

Oh, no!

They tried to make dinner.

But all they made was a big mess!

The next morning, Stuart, George,
Martha, and Mr. Little
took a good look around.

18

"Icky!" said Martha.

Just then, the phone rang.

It was great news.

"Our house is a finalist for

'Home of the Year!' " Stuart said.

Then Stuart broke the bad news.

The judges were coming over *that day*!

They needed to clean up fast!

"The only way to do a job this big

is to think like a Little!" said Stuart.

So that's what they did.

Even Snowbell helped out.

They cleaned the kitchen.

They tidied up the terrace.

They polished.

And they dusted.

They did it all the Little way!

Before long, the doorbell rang.

The judges were there!

Stuart and George met them at the door.

Mrs. Little was feeling better.

She came down to say hello.

"Welcome to our home!" she said.

"And what a lovely home it is,"

said Judge Betty.

"So neat and clean!"

The judges liked it so much,

it won "Home of the Year!"

"Now tell us," Judge Betty
said to Mrs. Little,
"what's your secret?"

Mrs. Little smiled.

"A *Little* help goes a long way!" she said.